WELCOME TO
PASSPORT TO READING
A beginning reader's ticket to a brand-new world!

Every book in this program is designed to build read-along and read-alone skills, level by level, through engaging and enriching stories. As the reader turns each page, he or she will become more confident with new vocabulary, sight words, and comprehension.

These PASSPORT TO READING levels will help you choose the perfect book for every reader.

READING TOGETHER
Read short words in simple sentence structures together to begin a reader's journey.

READING OUT LOUD
Encourage developing readers to sound out words in more complex stories with simple vocabulary.

READING INDEPENDENTLY
Newly independent readers gain confidence reading more complex sentences with higher word counts.

READY TO READ MORE
Readers prepare for chapter books with fewer illustrations and longer paragraphs.

This book features sight words from the educator-supported Dolch Sight Words List. This encourages the reader to recognize commonly used vocabulary words, increasing reading speed and fluency.

For more information, please visit passporttoreadingbooks.com.

Enjoy the journey!

Little, Brown and Company
Hachette Book Group
1290 Avenue of the Americas, New York, NY 10104
Visit us at LBYR.com

First Edition: November 2018

Little, Brown and Company is a division of Hachette Book Group, Inc.
The Little, Brown name and logo are trademarks of Hachette Book Group, Inc.

The publisher is not responsible for websites (or their content)
that are not owned by the publisher.

Library of Congress Control Number: 2018955137

ISBNs: 978-0-316-41377-0 (pbk.), 978-0-316-41376-3 (ebook),
978-0-316-41379-4 (ebook), 978-0-316-41378-7 (ebook)

Printed in the United States of America

CW

10 9 8 7 6 5

Passport to Reading titles are leveled by independent reviewers applying the
standards developed by Irene Fountas and Gay Su Pinnell in *Matching Books
to Readers: Using Leveled Books in Guided Reading*, Heinemann, 1999.

SPIDER-MAN
INTO THE SPIDER-VERSE

MEET THE NEW SPIDER-MAN

ADAPTED BY
RORY KEANE

LITTLE, BROWN AND COMPANY
New York   Boston

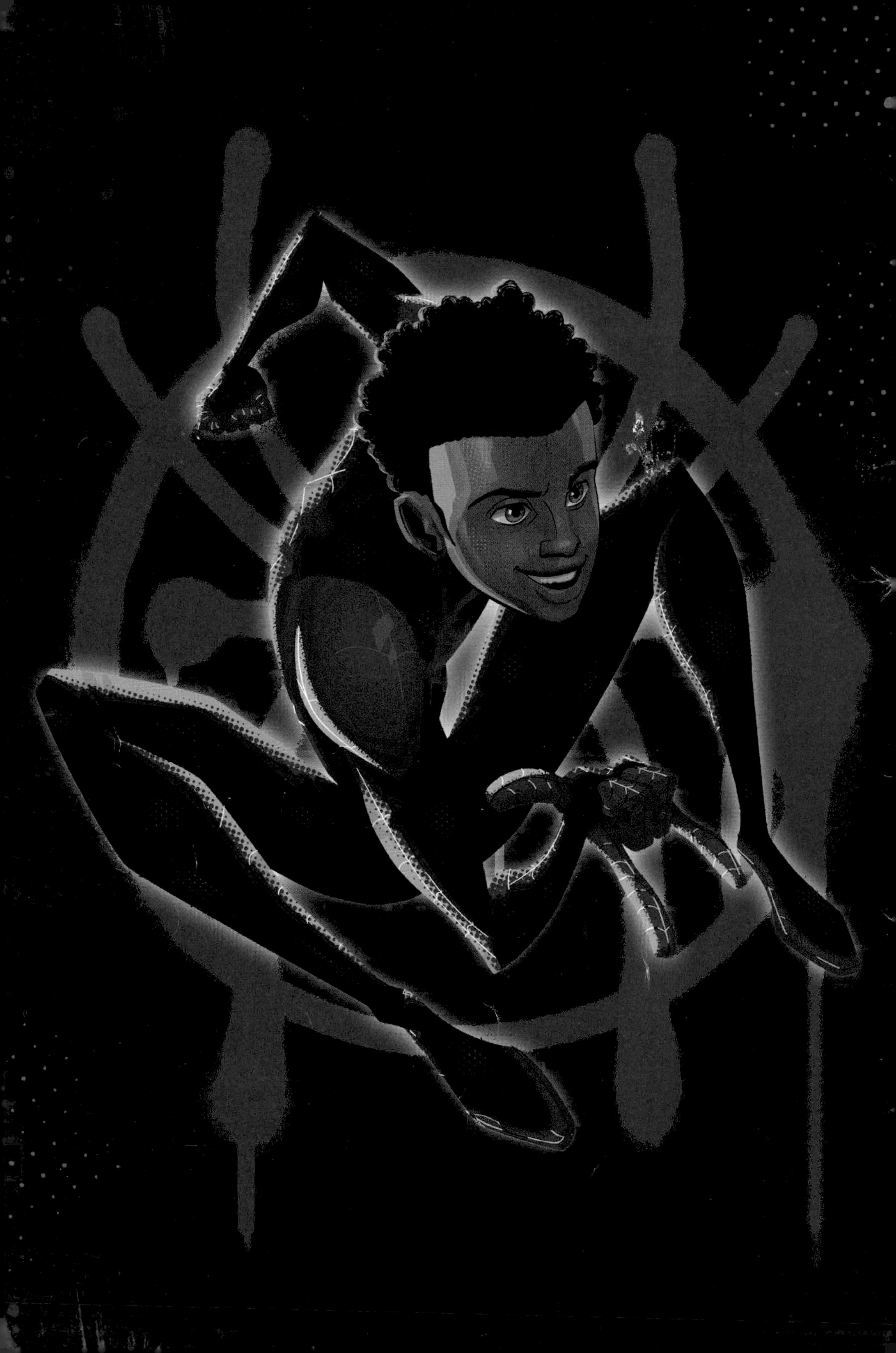

Attention, SPIDER-MAN fans!
Look for these words when you read
this book. Can you spot them all?

police officer

comic books

spray paint

costume

This is Miles Morales.
He lives in Brooklyn with
his parents, Jefferson and Rio.

Miles loves his parents,
even when his dad, Jefferson,
embarrasses him.
Jefferson is a police officer.
Rio is a nurse.

Miles is attending a new school this year. He feels lucky because it is a very good school, but he misses his old friends.

Miles is having a hard time
making new friends.
His roommate, Ganke,
does not talk to him.
Ganke likes to read comic
books instead.

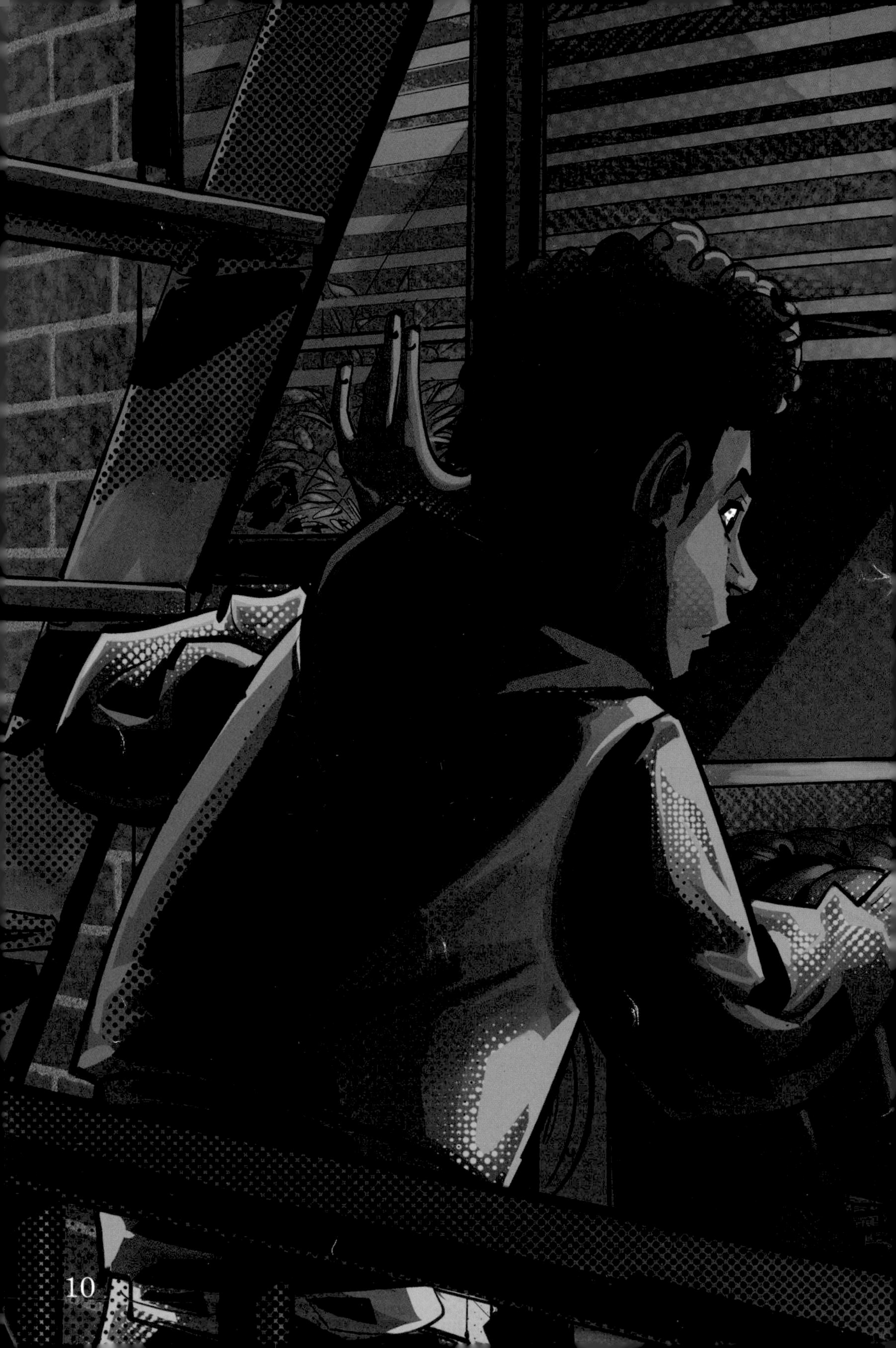

Miles goes to visit his
Uncle Aaron to feel better.
Uncle Aaron is Jefferson's brother.
Jefferson does not get along with
his brother anymore.

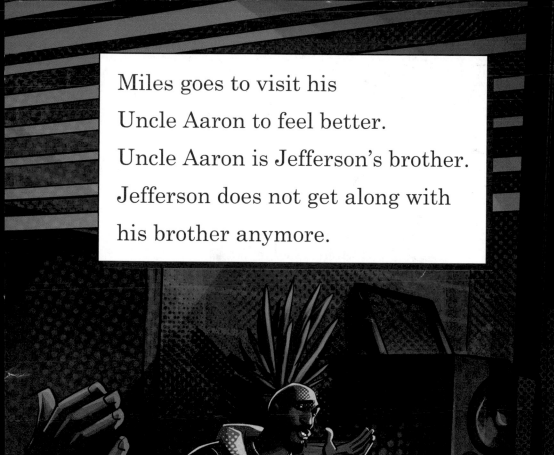

But Miles loves his uncle.
They hang out whenever they can.

Aaron takes Miles to a subway tunnel, where Miles has to climb a tall fence.

Aaron can hop over the fence easily.
Miles has a hard time climbing it.
Uncle Aaron laughs at Miles.

Uncle Aaron takes him to
spray paint at night.
Jefferson would be very mad
at Miles if he found out.

Aaron shows Miles a huge
empty wall that Miles can paint.
Miles loves making art.

While Miles is painting,
he does not see the spider
climbing down its web.

Oh no!
The spider bites Miles!
"AAAAAHHHHH!"

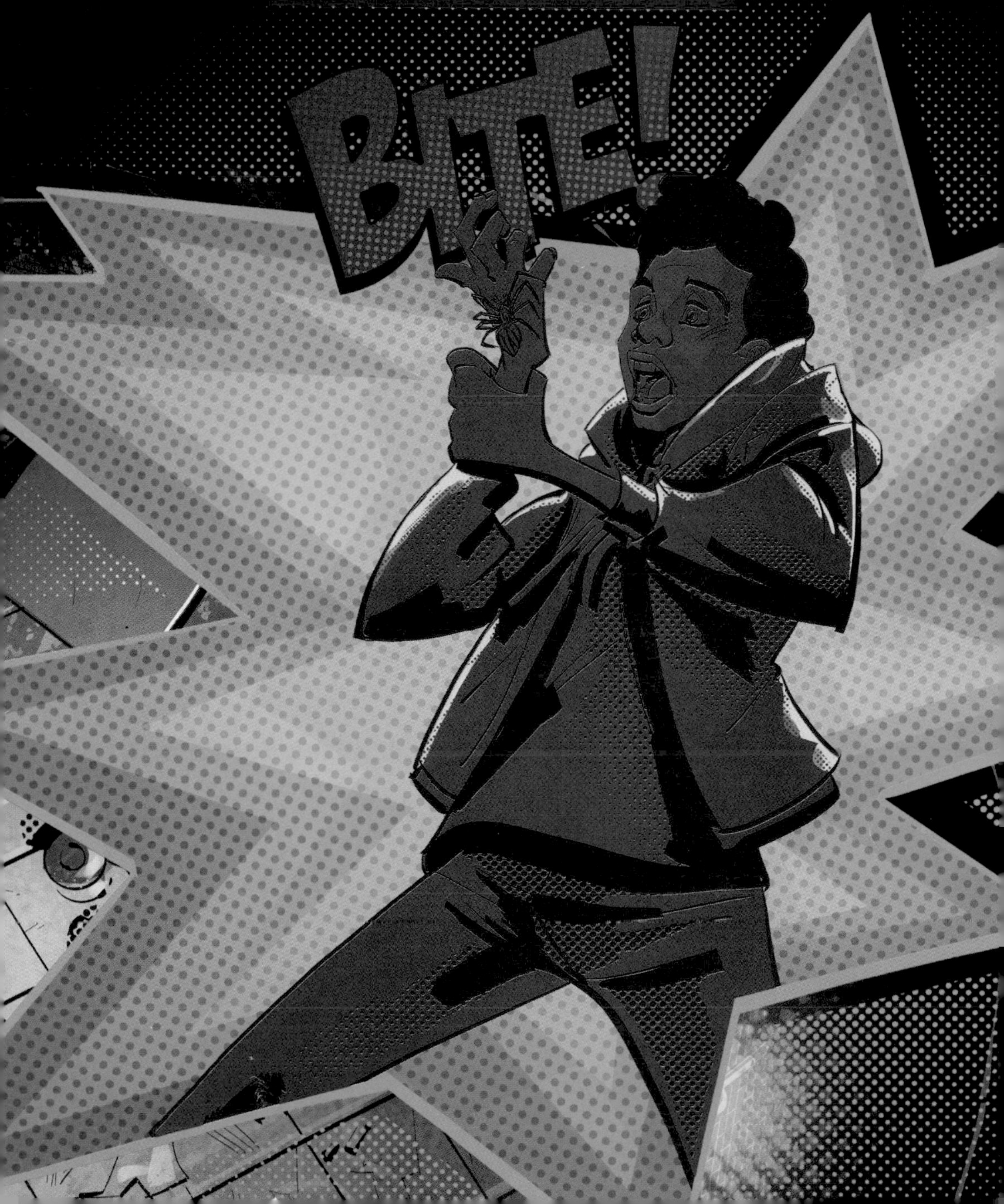
BITE!

The spider bite hurts.

Miles says he is fine.

Uncle Aaron takes him home.

The next day, Miles's pants are too short.
He grew overnight!
Something weird is definitely happening to Miles.

Miles sees his friend Wanda in the school hallway.

He says hi and touches
her shoulder.
And...

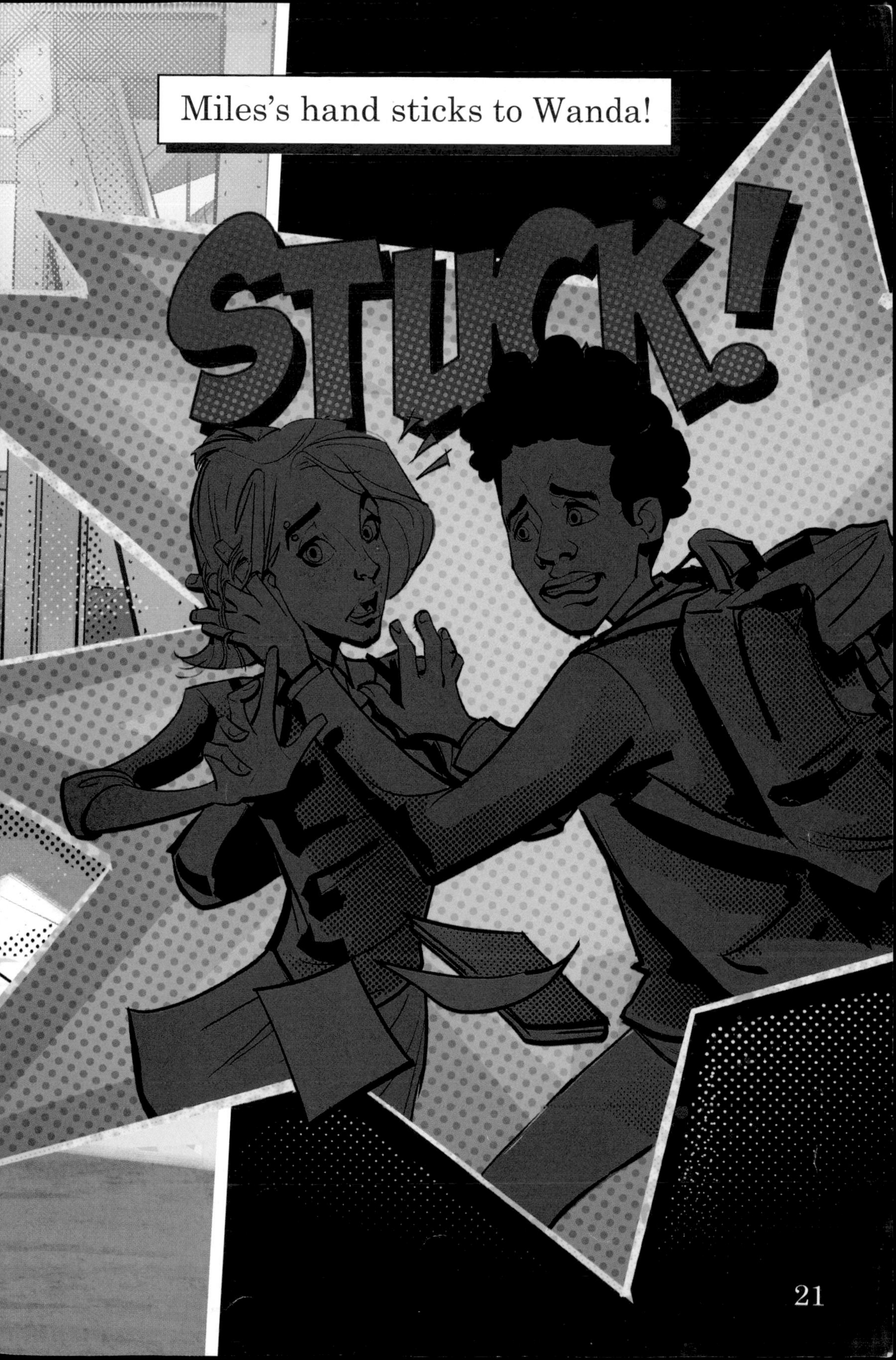
Miles's hand sticks to Wanda!
STUCK!

Miles tries to unstick his hand, but he accidentally makes it worse. A big crowd gathers to see what happened.

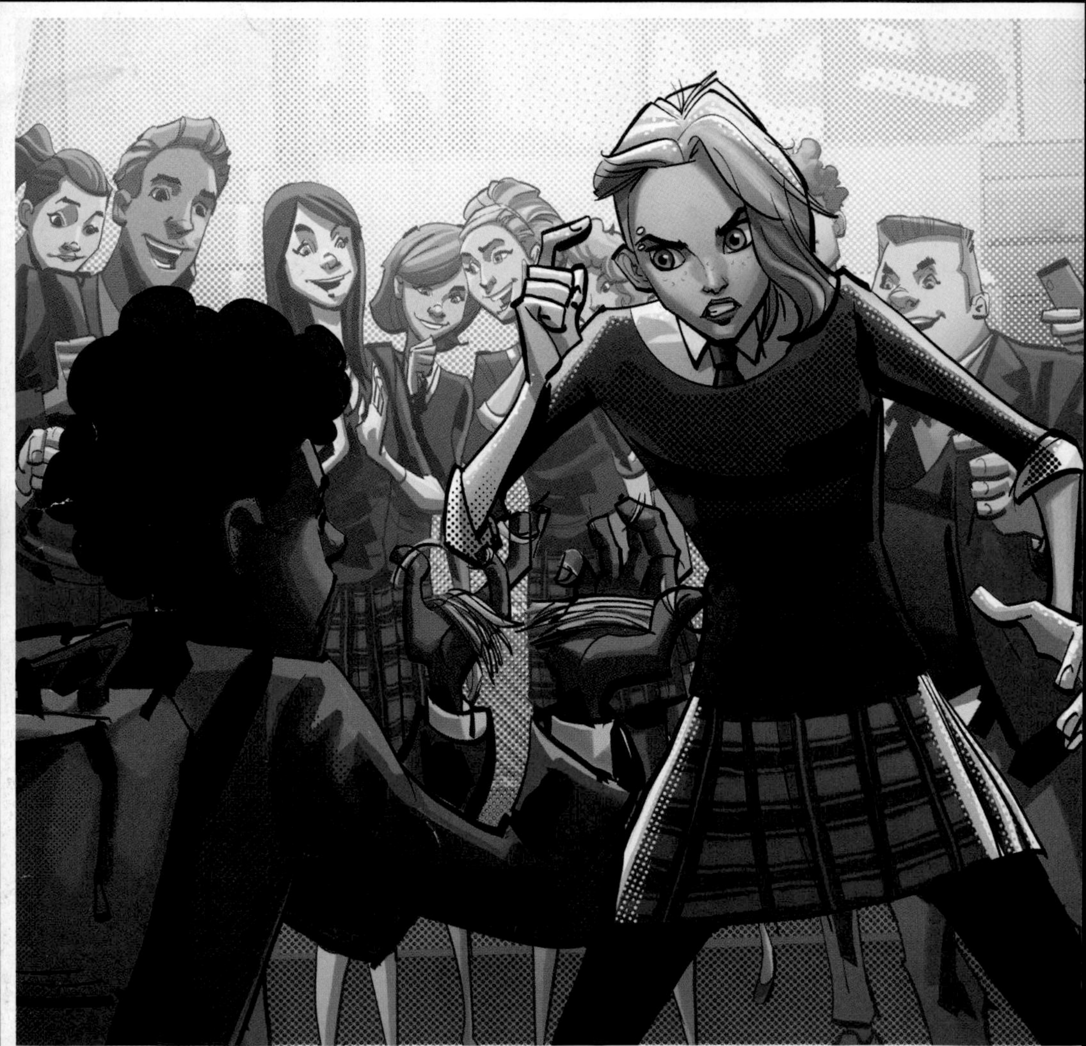

Miles pulls out some
of Wanda's hair!
He feels awful.
Wanda is very upset.

Miles runs away from Wanda
and the crowd.
He goes back to his room.
Then Miles sticks to his door....

He sticks to everything in his room.
He makes a big mess!

"Why is this happening?!" Miles yells.

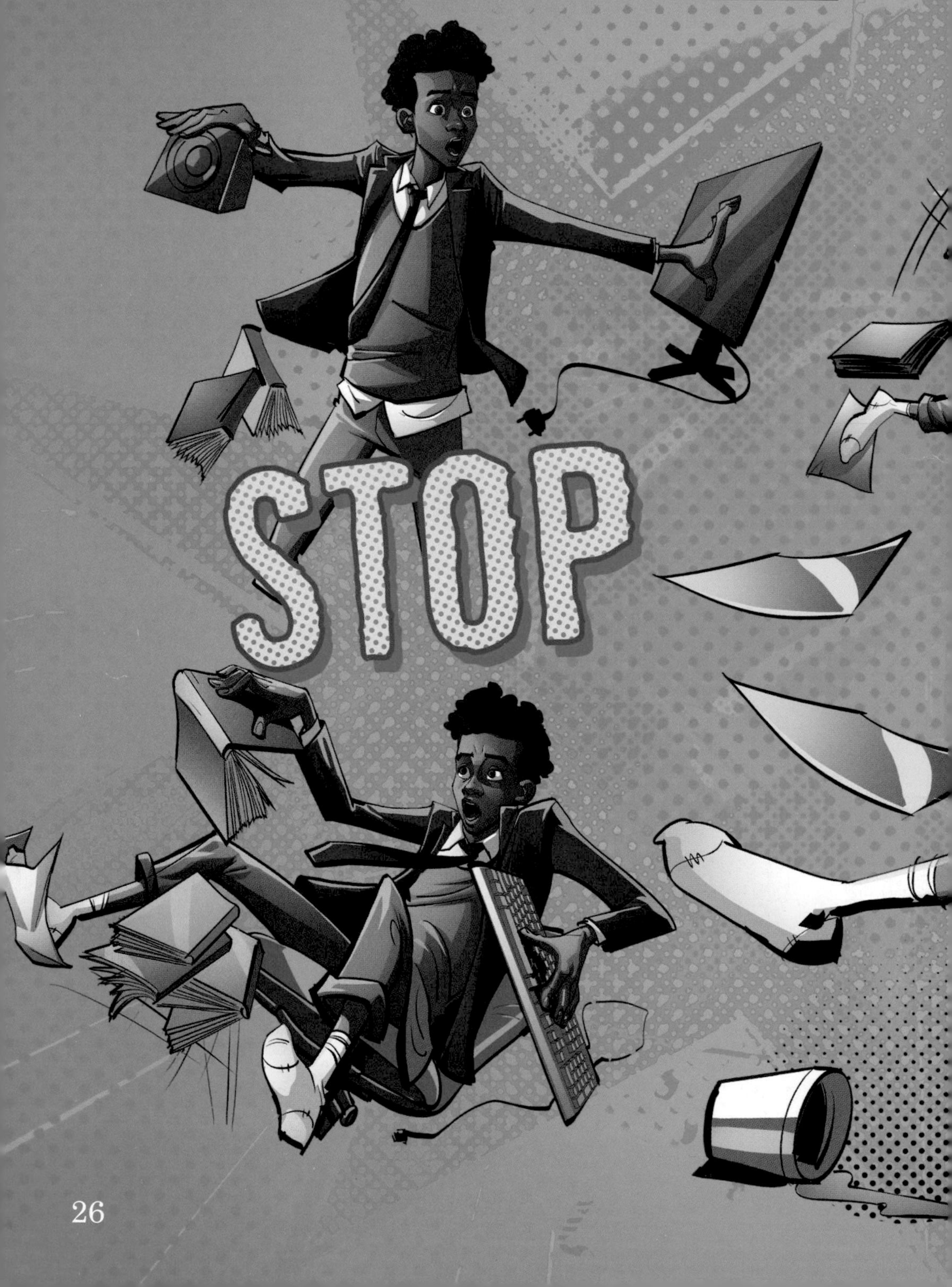
STOP

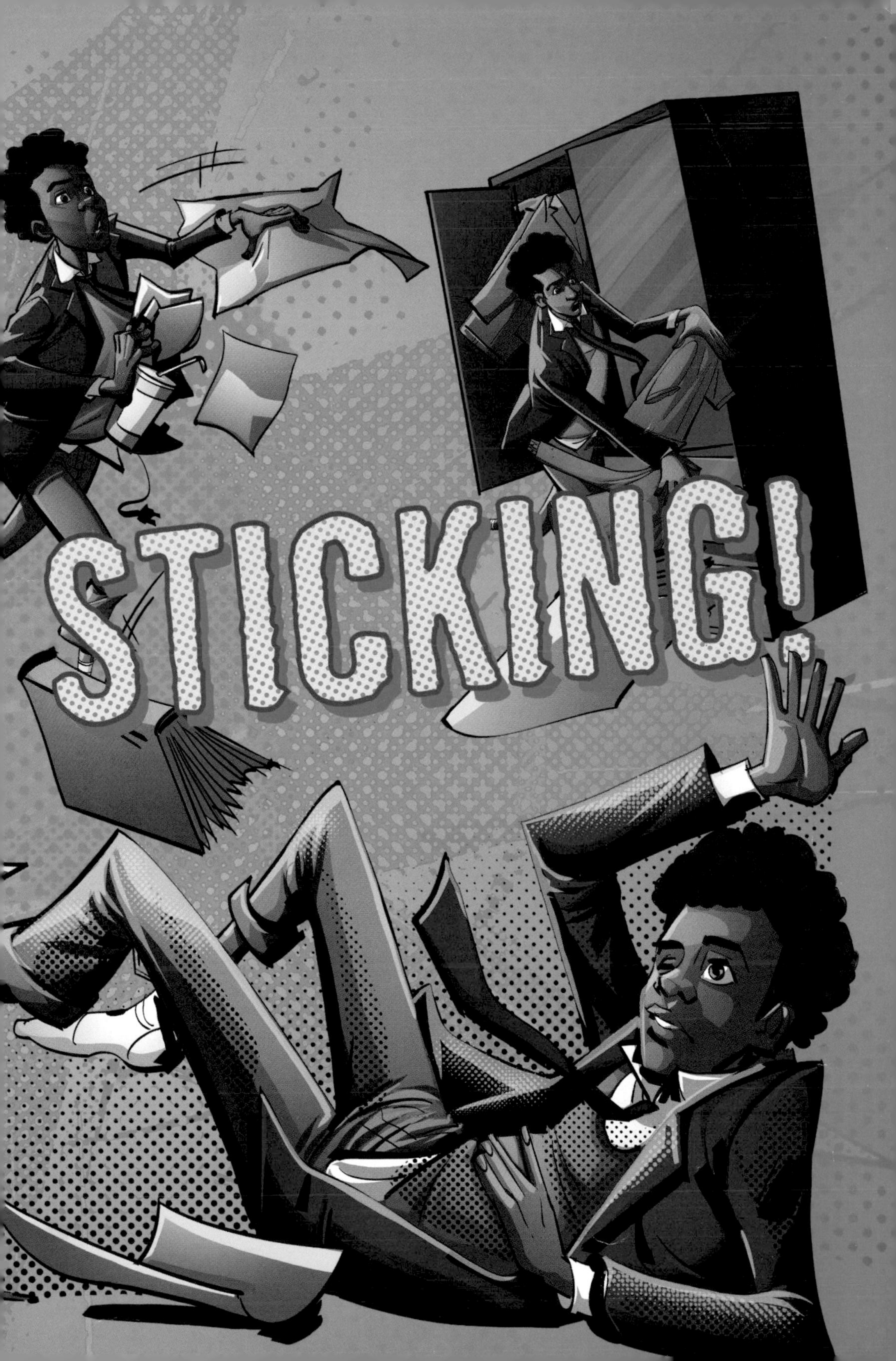
STICKING!

Miles lays on the floor.

One of Ganke's comic books falls on him.

"Oh no," Miles says.

It is a Spider-Man comic book.

The comic book gives Miles an idea.

Miles goes to the costume store.

He is looking for a Spider-Man outfit.

Miles puts on his disguise
and climbs a building.

His sticky hands are great for climbing!

He gets to the roof and looks out at Brooklyn.

A lot of weird things are happening, and Miles does not know why.

Could Miles be a brand-new Spider-Man? His new powers are still so confusing!

Miles needs all the help he can get if he wants to save the day like Spidey!